The FEARLESS PRINCESS and The Rescue Dogs

Bill Wilson

Treaty Oak Publishers

PUBLISHER'S NOTE

This is a work of fiction. All of the characters, business establishments, and events are based on the author's imagination. Any resemblance or similarity to persons, living or dead, or to business establishments, is unintentional and purely a coincidence.

Images by Bill Wilson
Cover design by Kim Greyer

Printed and published in the United States of America

TREATY OAK PUBLISHERS

ISBN: 978-1-943658-36-7

Available from Amazon

DEDICATION

For my daughter.
My strong girl, my sweet miracle, my fearless princess!

The FEARLESS PRINCESS and The Rescue Dogs

TABLE OF CONTENTS

Chapter 1

The Kingdom

G

In the old Kingdom of Greywood
We find young Goldie Vee,
Feeling humdrum and glum
Among some unremarkable things.

Atop her perched position,
The princess saw plain
A kingdom without color.
I mean, even its name was mundane.

A dull stone castle
Betwixt a small toneless town,
With frowning drab cottages
Stashed on ashen slate ground.

Whispers and claims
As legend explains
That a long time ago
During the festive springtime parades

Came an outsider in
Infiltrating around
And snaked Greywood's heart,
Then sneaked from the town.

No ordinary heart,
’Twas the prized Prism Stone.
Bestowing lustrous light
Bright and brilliant, it glowed.

With a flash on Lightning Ridge,
A blazing rainbow crashed.
And from the fiery comets blast
The Prism Stone came to pass.

The Stone brought abundance,
Growing emerald green grass,
Giant coral Maples and
Trumpet Honeysuckle plants.

Pink Wisteria trees hung
Strung, like cotton candy cheer,
Sheer heaven to sway under
Like a wondrous chandelier.

But when the Prism Stone vanished
The light in time did fade
And the dark-hearted King
Seemed to welcome the grey.

The King banned the band
And planned a town meet.
Each person was clammed
As the King gave his speech.

The KING'S WORDS

"We must stay diligent.
Nay, we must stay alert!
Foregoing silly distractions,
The town's safety comes first
We must stay diligent.
Nay, we must stay alert!
Fun, feelings, or festivals
Shan't interfere with our work."

And with that speech,
Happiness went amiss,
As the air grew sick
From the three rules he had picked.

Rule #1 – NO FESTIVALS

Until further notice, all celebrations, such as banquets, balls, birthday bashes, blow-outs, and backyard barbeques, are hence forth banned.

Rule #2 - NO FEELINGS

Until further notice, frivolous displays of emotion, such as smiles, smirks, giggles, and grins, shall cease. Including, but not limited to, bawling, bellyaching, blubbering, whimpering, weeping, and/or wailing.

Rule #3 – NO FUN

Until further notice, all merriment and amusement, fribble, fiddle-faddle, and frippery will, frankly, not be tolerated.

The great gates that once welcomed
Were covered with stone.
Sewn shut with mortar
As the King sat on his throne.

No more stores of dandy candy.
    Games were given the boot and canned
        No more chewy dew drops.
            Only boring chores were planned.

And so it was, over time
That the fine folks forgot
About laughter and play
And doing the things people ought.

The devious and wicked King
Grimaced in the grim
For the kingdom outside
Now matched his darkness within.

But, as with any power,
In time it is spent.
The wretched King passed,
And kings came and went.

But new rulers had no knowledge
Of beauty and bright things.
Thus the fiendish plot endured,
A diseased dismal scheme.

Centuries passed
And the three laws stayed.
Decay befell Greywood,
As it could not help but fade.

Twisted vines strained
And overcame the town wall,
But no one dared change,
Strangely, no one at all.

That is, until one day
Inquired a keen Goldie Vee,
"Why does no one question
The Three Rule Decree?"

You see, young Goldie Vee
Didn't quite grasp status quo.
A "just because" reply
Was a worse answer than "no."

Her family politicked,
Prim, proper, and slick,
But Goldie Vee would admit
She was quite opposite.

She had her own style.
Maybe clothing choices lacked,
She couldn't coordinate much of anything.
Even her eyes didn't match.

Scorned for too much imagination,
Laughed at for being too tall,
Only her dad said kind things,
But you know…Kings are busy and all.

So she kept to herself.
She knew she didn't fit in.
With no real place in the house,
The outdoors was her friend.

Exploring the kingdom
And mapping the land,
She knew each nook and cranny
Like the back of her hand.

She was incurably inquisitive
Eager as a young girl could be
But for all her knowledge she couldn't predict
Where her curiosity might lead.

Chapter 2

An Adventure Begins

DANGER
DO NOT CLIMB!
NO

One evening out exploring
Per her post-homework routine,
Goldie Vee spotted a creature
Like nothing she'd seen.

Now naturally that's not saying
Or conveying a whole lot,
Considering all she had seen
Was a grey hound and a grey fox.

But, awed, she crept closer,
Drew nearer for a clear sight.
Then the purple creature spied her
And vanished into the night.

A disappointing outcome.
She knew she must pursue,
But her Auntie looked up
And with a scolding rebuke

Gave a sermon on savages,
An oration on ogres.
“Only beasts, brutes, and thieves
Lie over our borders.”

That night, Goldie Vee pondered
As she lay down in bed,
Paying no attention to the warning,
She wandered off in her head.

A world wide open
With new adventure to explore,
This land of myth called.
She just must see more.

Again, forgetting her Auntie's
Extravagant critique,
She slunk out the next morning
For another sneak peek.

Now next to the wall
Craning her neck, looking up
She thought, *I can climb this.*
Just a hop, skip, and a jump.

So on the count of three,
Goldie Vee scrambled up quick
But prickly stick branches
got her stuck in a pinch.

Nearly halfway up,
her doubts set in.
As her nerves gave out,
the ground geared up to spin.

Snagging her grey garb
On a thorny thistle barb,
She lost her sharp focus
And came crashing down hard.

A sting shot up her arm,
As she let out a scream,
Howling from the pain
Like a whistling pot of hot steam.

Chapter 3

GIVE UP, GOLDIE VEE!

Now grounded forever
with sisters flaunting her flop,
Goldie Vee, haunted by failure,
decided to stop.

She'd quit exploring wonder
and be more like the others.
Tired from blunders –
she stopped dreaming in color.

Ignoring the light outside,
She'd live in the grey,
Only watching the shadows
From inside her cave.

Seasons changed
And she almost forgot
'Bout strange unknown creatures
And her preposterous plot.

With life back to normal,
Formal, boring, and plain,
She stayed inside mostly
Avoiding her old outdoor ways.

The castle RN
called Goldie Vee in
For one final check
Regarding her arm on the mend.

Rolling up Goldie Vee's sleeve,
The nurse was happy to reveal
"Your arm is all better.
Looks like it's finally healed."

It was the best news Goldie Vee
Had heard in a while.
With a slight pep in her step,
She almost accidentally smiled.

She was eager to tell
Her dad the good news,
But as she got close to his office
She stopped, all confused.

As she overheard the town doctor,
Who talked in a grave solemn way,
Say, "You are sick, my King.
I give you a week to ten days.

"This is an illness unlike
anything I have seen.
The disease is spreading too fast.
I am sorry, my King."

Her aunt burst out crying.
And now her own tears would fall,
About to betray her position,
Previously hidden in the hall.

So she turned and ran,
Trying to distance the pain.
She needed her dad!
How could he leave her this way?

Trying to outrun the hurt,
Her speed smearing tears,
The doctors words rang
And clanged in her ears.

She could always find peace in the trees.
The woods would ease the pain.
But no peace was found
As dark clouds brought the rain.

Feeling defeated,
She sat teary-eyed and sad
On the last green patch of grass.
Life had cheated her dad.

A frail and worn lady
Approached Goldie Vee,
Her eyes understanding
As she took a sod seat.

Goldie Vee had seen
This elderly lady before
In a wilting maple grove
By the gate to the North.

School kids conjured
    Wild stories of a witch.
        "Idle chatter and nonsense,"
            Goldie Vee would then answer their lip.

A croaking voice spoke,
"Child, why do you cry?"
"I'm not crying!" Goldie Vee shouted
In a poignant reply.

"But I see no rule police,
It's okay if we weep."
"It's my father," then sobbed Goldie Vee.
"The doctor only gave him a week."

The elderly lady surged with urgency
Asking, "One doctor?" "Some surgeon?"
"Why, child, does your version
Place all hope in one person?

"Hope's found all around
But 'tis best to begin
Not to your left nor your right,
Rather finding hope from within."

Then the lady sighed,
And shut her knowing eyes
And told Goldie Vee
Of the old wicked king's lies.

"As previously believed
The Prism Stone was not thieved.
But it was the old king by whom
the kingdom was deceived.

"He hid the stone away
To bring sadness and woe
So the town would need him
Instead of the bright Prism Stone.

"His jealousy made him sick
And darkness crept in.
It spread slowly, unknowingly,
Choking all life from within.

"The crops and trees died
From bleakness and thirst.
At last the people got sick,
And her father was first.

"There is but only one way
to fix this foul fate.
Retrieve the Prism Stone posthaste
Before it's too late."

Then she reached out slowly
And dropped a few broken bits
Of brilliant stone fragments
Into Goldie Vee's grip.

"Shards of the Rainbow Comet
From which the Prism Stone came.
When you're close, you will know.
They will guide you and light the way."

Goldie Vee studied the pieces
Then stood up from the ground.
But when she scanned for the lady,
Not a soul was around.

She trudged home, reeling,
Feeling like an elephant's foot
And stared down at her shoes
with a malevolent look.

Rancorous and resentful
Vehemently bitter
Begrudgingly venomous
Intently full of vinegar.

Angry at her dumb family.
Angry at herself and this dumb town.
But her anger was just sadness
Bottled up and pushed down.

She would show everyone
That she was capable of doing things right!
"I'll save Greywood myself
And I'll do it tonight!"

Chapter 4

ALL OR NOTHING

Now the sun,
recently deceased,
Beseeches the Moon
For rebirth in the East.

And so frees Eve,
Giving her brief reprieve
In guarding day from night.
Allowing the moon's release

With obscurity now seized,
A raspy wind wheezed.
Bullying frail trees
While shadows take feast

But ’tween nicely creased sheets,
The towns’ people did sleep.
Except poor Goldie Vee wouldn’t,
Couldn’t find any peace.

Her nerves made her sweat
As she fluttered by fret.
Yet her mind was made up
So she took that first step.

Slowly tip-toe’dly,
Goldie Vee crept.
Opening the window,
Adeptly she trekked.

’Round the sleeping village,
Down a calculated road,
She trod on with moxie
And promptly made her approach.

Retracing her steps,
She spotted and spied
This polished purple creature.
And narrowing her eyes,

Launched over the hedge
Headlong into the brush,
Quickly twisting and bending,
Her mission a must!

Jolted, the creature saw
Then bolted and reversed.
Immersed in pursuit,
Goldie Vee bounded and burst.

The thistle scraped
And gave a miserable gash.
Anxiously she watched
As the creature slid down a crack.

Then skipped through the wall.
Now's her last chance!
It's all or nothing!
As she made a mad dash,

She realized the hole
Was too small for her to fit.
But kicking some rocks loose, she thought,
If I squeeze in a bit…

She drew a sharp breath
Holding it in tight.
She must break through.
Only CAN, there's no TRY!

With all the might she could muster
She pushed at the stone,
And seconds later she broke through
to the new, the unknown.

Instantly she was tumbling
Into a jumbled confusion
As her momentum carried her forward
Careening against crumbling protrusions.

As she rose up from the gravel
She said, "What have I done?
I can't believe that I'm here!"
Wherever here is, she thought, stunned

Now this place was quite new.
And new can be scary,
Because new is different,
And *different* is *daring.*

But strong-willed and unyielding,
She dusted the hair from her face
And took an unfamiliar path
In this bewildering place.

Chapter 5

A New Land

Exactly eight steps later,
Or maybe seven - No, it was nine.
Whatever it was - not important,
'Twas a pleasant surprise.

Because she came nose to nose,
Or should I say nose to snout,
And at last met the sneaky beast
She had wondered about!

This creature's features were
All orange and purple.
Goldie Vee stood speechless as it spoke
With its bizarre foreign verbal.

Then the creature with a gurgle
Cleared his throat and might have sung.
"Why, I do declare,
That bad cat had my tongue!"

You, you…can speak like me?"
Goldie Vee stammered.
"Yes, oh yes…"
He rang out, with a pleased gleeful clamor.

"But you're a dog," she giggled,
"And dogs usually can't converse."
"Well, I am a rescue dog
And I'm lettered in poem and verse.

"So I see why you're here,
My companion, my friend.
We rescue dogs get saved
But save our friends in the end."

"Of course, with regrets,
Rescue dogs don't always have friends.
Our mixed profile, you could say,
Doesn't help us fit in.

"We're not the status-quo,
You know…of what a proper dog should be.
Rescue dogs are 'all the same'
And we're just 'always mean.'

"But our differences are our strengths.
We'll go to great lengths to prove
Our love for our families,
And our family's friends, too."

Goldie Vee's mind whirled
And ticked like a blinker,
As the words the dog spoke
Twirled and smacked in her thinker.

Then she asked wherc she was.
He said, "Where you're at.
You are where I am,
And I'll leave it at that.

"Now travel, head west
You'll find what you seek.
Oh, and I almost forgot
There's just one last little thing:

"Beware, Beware
Of the Lamina Lortnoc's steel snare
Be wary and cautious
Or you'll disappear forever, I swear!"

Then with a kind parting lick,
A slobbery kiss to the face,
He disappeared quick.
Poof, without even a trace.

So traveling on,
Goldie Vee wasted no time.
She made a left at the bridge
At a quarter 'til nine.

Here she found a hound
With a candy pink tongue
Who was barking at bats
Saying goodnight to the sun.

With a wink and smile,
He woofed her a greeting.
"Hi," said the princess.
"A marvelous meeting!"

"I see you're searching,
Missing love," he said.
"Yes, but how did—"
He held up his paw.
"On your face - like a book that I've read"

Then with a carriage of caring
He launched his soliloquy,
Whence forth came
A soft lyrical epiphany.

"In fact, the lack of love
Does lead to a lackluster life.
So don't wait for love to fade
Before you search for love's light.

"Love morning and night.
Love all during the day.
Love keeps us healthy
And sweeps away the grey."

Just then...

Squish-Squash, Squish-Squash!
The mysterious sound drew near.
Shhh…Lortnocs… Lortnocs…
A serious warning rang in her ear.

Squish-Squash, Squish-Squash!
The Lortnocs stepped in their galoshes,
A hodge podge of grumbling noises,
As if purposefully obnoxious.

The Noise grew faint again…

"Whew! That was close,"
The hound sounded off.
"Yes, too close for comfort
For us traveling dogs."

Then under a star-filled sky,
He said, "It's my time to fly."
And with his paw in hand
She shook it goodbye.

Continuing her journey...

With the bright morning sun
Lightly warming her now,
She eyed a large shape
and raising her brow,

Spied a gigantic dog
With a single spot huge and blue,
Who howled at Goldie Vee,
"How do you doooo?"

"Not so great, I'm afraid,"
Said young Goldie Vee.
"I need to hurry home
To save my father, the King."

"I see," said the pup.
"May I lend a helping paw?"
"Can you point me toward the Prism Stone?"
Said Goldie Vee. "Is it far?"

"Hmm, I've heard that old story,
The crazed grey king and what not.
But I don't know the way,
Since everyone here has forgot."

"I understand," said Goldie Vee.
"And please excuse my poor manners.
I haven't asked you how you're doing,
Just overwhelmed you with my answers."

"Well, to be perfectly honest,
I don't like my big spot."
And he added sadly,
"My friends laugh a whole lot.

"I wished it on my back,
But it stuck to my face."
"Well, I think it's perfect,"
Goldie Vee said.
"Yes, perfectly placed."

"Why, thank you, princess,
For that kindness you told,
I could tell you are brave
Because *kindness* is *bold*."

Then with a hug and wag
The two soon parted.
With no time to waste
A path Goldie Vee charted.

As she walked and worried
The clouds thickened around.
The wind quickened swiftly,
And her smile turned to a frown.

Suddenly...

Blowing and blasting
A squall came to life stewing.
She cried, "Oh, dear!
A fuss must be brewing."

But with a baritone bark,
A dog said, "Stay calm.
Don't worry about a thing
And try my shades on."

She slipped on the glasses
And everything changed.
She was standing in the sun
A day with no rain.

"Ah, yes," he said.
"I see your head's leaning.
'Tis the lens we look through
That gives us our meaning."

The smile then returned
  To Goldie Vee's mouth.
    A good friend always helps
      To overcome doubt.

And so with a curtsy,
And a returned bow-wow bow,
Goldie Vee continued her journey
With time running out.

Creeping distantly deeper,
Up steep hills all day,
  She heard *squish-squash* behind her,
Just a hair's breadth away.

Frozen, like a ship
Anchored firmly to the sea floor,
Goldie Vee couldn't move.
The chains of fear had her moored.

Then her legs knocked
  And out gave her knees.
    As a lunging Lortnoc swiped,
        Goldie Vee slipped, tripped down a ravine.

Chapter 6

LOST

Shook, a bit hazy
Dazed, but okay,
She found herself stuck
In a subterranean cave

Knowing she was trapped,
She wished to scream out in a panic.
But with her dubious surroundings,
She settled for a quiet, "Dagnabit!"

Through the damp dark ducts,
The air struck her senses,
As the cloaked chill of the cavern
Made her intensely apprehensive.

With her imagination working feverishly,
She kept a tight leash on her mind,
Ignoring notions of giant rats
Or voracious bats of the kind.

"Oh, I must get out!
  I haven't got time for this.
    I must escape
      From this dismal abyss."

She sprinted through the cavern
In a frantic busy sweat
In a tizzy with no direction.
Dizzy and defeated she wept.

Weary from her plight,
She slumped against a stone.
  "I can't do anything right.
  "I should've stayed home."

Surrendering to the scarcity,
Her grievous breathing curtailed.
In this moment, there was nothing,
Nada, the Princess had failed.

AND SO...

The silent dystopia was ready
to start its victory lap
The darkness had won.
Offering no second chance

But impolitely interrupted,
The shadows were shoved back
By the happiest of things,
A wagging tail in her lap.

Cancelling her trance,
He chortled, "How do you do?"
As this red dog appeared
From out of the blue.

He gazed at her
And she looked at him,
Inspiring a smile,
An instantaneous friend.

SHE SAID...

"Hey, Mr. Red Dog,
Are you stuck in here, too?"
"No, I've been waiting to greet you,
As rescue dogs always do.

"We wait in excited patience
For our best friends to be near.
Then offer a wagging tail
And lend two floppy ears.

"So tell me what ails you,
Sweet Goldie Vee.
I'll snuggle up close
while you share your worries with me."

GOLDIE VEE EXPLAINED...

"I've always struggled to do…
Well, I guess, to *be* like the rest.
See, when I think - it's different
And my mind insists this is best.

"I bet my sisters could've done this.
Found the Prism Stone with ease,
Then my dad would be saved.
Life for them is a breeze."

GOLDIE VEE STILL RANTED...

"I'm too tall for my desk.
Kids snicker and squeak,
And I'm always picked last
When we play - work and go seek."

"I hear what you're saying
And it sounds like you're in pain.
Conflicted to be normal,
But wanting love just the same.

"But lucky for you,
I know a secret about life.
And you're about to find out
And get perspective on why.

"You see, it all means
Quite simply, *diddly squat.*
I know it's painful now, but soon
Zilch, zero and zot!"

SO I TELL YOU...

"Think differently, Goldie Vee.
Be indifferent to what they think.
Choose your pursuit with purpose,
Deem your *difference* - your *strength*,

"Think differently, Goldie Vee.
The difference is how you think.
Be intentional to effect change.
Persistence is all you need."

When the Red Dog finished
  His words sunk in bit by bit.
    It made sense to Goldie Vee,
      You could say the shoe fit.

And now that her tears were gone
And feelings of panic had left,
She thought differently about her situation.
Simply what she did best.

She remembered the fragments
The frail lady once gave
And when she pulled them out
They cast a dim light in the cave.

As she scanned and analyzed,
She saw it wasn't a real cave at all.
This place was man-made,
The floors, ceilings, and walls.

Think, Goldie Vee.
This seems eerily familiar.
Who would build such a place?
An obscure lurid lair.

Think, Think, Goldie Vee.
Yes, yes, that must be it!
A despairingly dark place
Is where the Prism Stone is hid.

How would you design a place?
Now thought Goldie Vee,
If you were a self-absorbed,
Narcissistic old king?

She wondered aloud, "Hmmm....
Egotistical and callous?
Eureka! I would design it
Like my own private palace.

"My map's in my sachel!"
She rushed for her scrolls
As the fragments grew brighter
Anticipating their role.

"Ah hah, while my dad was busy
At a town hall luncheon,
I mapped the secret rooms
Reserved for only an official king function."

Then she got her bearings
And shouted to her friend,
"It's up two lefts and then right,
Then down to the end."

The fragments helped guide them
And at last they turned to see.
"Just a wall with cob webs," woofed Red Dog
As he looked at Goldie Vee.

"But check out my scribbles
That I drew on my map.
There were two sconces on the wall
And one was crooked and cracked."

She persisted in her efforts
And tugged at the webs,
When two sconces appeared,
Just like her map notes had read.

She took a chance
And pulled down on the fixture,
Cranking it 'round,
'Til the ancient piece splintered.

And with a deep growl,
The whole wall roared
Like a den of bickering lions.
Dust in chaos now soared.

But as the dust thinned,
Then lively light leaped.
It shimmied, then tangoed
And foxtrotted, cheek-to-cheek.

It bounced off the walls
And engulfed Goldie Vee.
It flickered with optic flavor
An exquisite visual feast.

"We've found the heart of Greywood!"
Shouted Goldie Vee.
"The Prism Stone is found.
This will fix the sick king!"

Drawn to its light,
She stood near to the stone.
"We can still save my dad.
It's time to go home!"

She stuffed it into her sack,
Packed like a soft loaf of bread.
"Now, let's get the lead out!"
As she patted Red Dog on the head.

With the cavern fully lit,
They saw a possible exit above,
But they'd have to climb the wall.
"Ugh!" she grumbled and shrugged.

Slow like cold syrup,
She stepped to the wall.
"Why do I have to climb again?
What if I slip and I fall?

"And then break my arm.
I'll be stuck here forever!"
"Walls are always in one's way,"
Said Red Dog. "You just have to be clever."

Flustered but determined
She mustered up her might.
From determined to focused,
She kept the top in her sight.

Her fingers found crevices
Between the large chiseled rock.
Her feet crammed in fissures,
Little retreats in the blocks.

As she made her ascent
Navigated near the top,
The walls became smooth
With no more grab-able spots.

She wished she had some rope.
As a lump welled up in her throat,
"I guess I'll have to jump,
Or else 'that's all she wrote'."

The fear was still there
But this time with no hesitation
She put that fear to use
As true motivation.

So with a *fearless* leap
Which is how leaps are perceived by others,
She soared through the cavern,
Stretching her limbs onward and upward.

Her fingers brushed soil
And found dangling tree roots.
She clenched her fists tightly rigid
Fighting nail and tooth.

With legs in tow
She pulled herself over and up
To safety, fresh air,
And the blue sky above.

She laughed out loud
With a burst of joyous awe,
Processing how she escaped
Doom's clutches and claws.

It was her *differences* after all
That helped her succeed.
Had she not loved to explore,
This success wouldn't be.

Had she not been so tall,
Five inches taller than her grade,
She would have failed at that jump,
Stuck in the cave, I'm afraid.

Her mouth couldn't help it,
Grinning like never before,
Just as up bounded Red Dog,
Boosting himself from the cave floor.

RED DOG SHOUTED...

"I knew you could make it!
I had no doubt you'd prevail
Because you chose what you wanted.
You set your course and you sailed!"

"Thank you again, Red Dog,
For believing in me.
I'd love for you to come back
And meet my father, the King."

"I'd love that, too," he said.
And the two journeyed back
Home to save the Kingdom
With the Prism Stone in her pack.

Chapter 7

Homeward Bound

Next they came upon
The Red Ruby Fields
Like candy coated apples
With delicious appeal.

THEN...

Startling her sharply
Something came into view.
And a dog appeared
With ears of bright blue.

He had huge teeth like a mammoth.
"EEK!" She stumbled back a step.
But then she thought,
Well, what'd you expect?

She had through her journey
Fondly came to possess
The idea that *different* isn't bad.
Quite the opposite, in fact - *Different is best!*

The three chatted and giggled
As the blue-eared dog wiggled.
His teeth were quite huge,
But his fierceness was little.

She hugged him goodbye.
But a ruckus abruptly struck
As a Lortnoc appeared,
Causing a wild rumpus to erupt.

Brouhaha insued.
The Lortnoc were hot on their trail
Henceforth came hallaballoo,
As pandemonium prevailed.

"Hark," howled Red Dog.
"The wall is in view."
"Phew!" said Goldie Vee.
"Let's hurry on through.

"Follow me to the crack.
We'll lose this Lortnoc there."
They made a B-line and dived in,
Escaping the snare by a hair.

As they blasted through the crack,
The Lortnoc walloped into the wall,
Irately clobbering with fists,
Since the crack was too small.

Chapter 8

HOME

Now safe back in Greywood
Where the journey began,
Goldie Vee looked for the lady
Who placed the rock shards in her hand.

She searched the spot
Where her home used to be
In the wilting maple grove,
But found nothing but trees.

Realizing time was almost up,
Her curiosity had to wait.
She raced toward the main square,
Shouting out the whole way,

"I found it!" Announcing again with pride,
"The heart of Greywood I found!
The town can be saved.
Now we're all safe and sound."

As she went to pull
The Prism prize from her pack
And attempted to hold it,
Her jaw dropped and went slack.

"What! But how?"
And now thinking back…
"Ugh! When I dashed from the Lortnoc
And crashed through the crack,

I thought it was the wall,
Yes, the wall that got broke,
But I guess I was wrong."
Dolefully choking up as she spoke,

"I guess it was the stone
I had placed in my pack
That against the wall thrashed,
Smacked hard and got smashed."

As she plowed closer to the plaza
Where a big crowd had gathered 'round
She noticed all heads low bowed.
"What's wrong? Why's the town looking down?"

Goldie Vee caught a glance
Of her mom's bereaved face.
Her mom shook her head
And Goldie Vee knew it was *too late*.

She pushed through the crowd.
Her dad can't be saved.
No one made a sound
With the three rules distinctly displayed.

Breaking the rules, she scowled
And howled with rage aloud,
A big *faux pas* as she defied the law
And screamed bitterly at the crowd,

"What's wrong with all of you?
My dad loved everyone here.
You stand like stumped statues do,
Looking stupefied in the mirror!"

As she placed the broken pieces down
On her dad's final resting place
She had that look of what could have been,
Like a royal flush less an ace.

On bended knees she whispered,
"I tried, Dad, I tried.
I'm sorry I can't hug you now.
I guess we ran out of time."

The crowd was in shock on this crowded block
By such emotion on display.
Everyone froze like Jack Frost's toes.
Even the breeze didn't ask the leaves to play.

This time she didn't care.
As tears welled up in her eyes,
Goldie Vee would not leave her dad.
She would not go run and hide.

Titanic teardrops of grief glinted
And streamed down her cheeks.
They splashed onto the fragmented rock
Of each small Prism piece.

The stone pieces glowed
As tears continued their cascade,
A composition of colors unfolded
That soon took center stage.

Washing away the dust of time,
Rinsing away woes
Repairing emotions of life and love,
Their brightness level rose.

Red and Yellow zip-zapped around,
While Indigo did go this way and that.
Blue hummed Violet a tune,
And Green and Orange rocked a dance.

Everyone cried or laughed.
But all were baffled by the light,
As each show of sentiment
Made the light shine thrice as bright.

Soon the crowd grew into a frenzy,
A fever pitch of feelings,
Until the dazzling twinkle gleamed
Beams so bright it was all-revealing.

The truth now lucid Goldie Vee saw.
If you want to determine how
Truly colorful a life you can live,
Then measure how much color you allow.

If you shut your life off to any risk,
And insist living safe and small,
You are shutting out the reward of joy
That comes with getting up after you fall.

All the town folk heard the message:
"Our light comes from love.
We don't need a Prism Stone to add color.
Just a wagging tail and hug."

Folks spun around in amazement.
The grass and trees came alive.
Even less gray hair on the old
And definitely more blue in the sky.

Sugar velvet Poppies bloomed
With sherbert Eucalyptus.
Such delicious combinations
Like blueberry-fruit Hibiscus.

The boiling roar of the crowd
Slowly simmered to a hush.
And all was silent once again
When a deep-warm voice spoke up.

"Goldie Vee, my girl."
She felt a soft touch on her chin
As a strong but gentle hand reached out
And tilted her head up to him.

"Your love brought light back in my life,
Saving a callous King from his fate,
Reviving my heart to feel again.
For love it's never too late.

"You saved the day and slayed the grey,"
Her dad said as he smiled down.
Then he kissed her on the head
And bestowed on her a perfect crown

"Alas, as King I have one last task."
And her dad stepped and pulled his sword.
Then with one precise and powerful blow
He proclaimed, "The three rules are no more!"

He picked his girl up and set her
On his shoulders for all to see.
"Let's hear three cheers for my hero,
For the Fearless Princess, Goldie Vee!"

About the Author

BILL WILSON

Bill Wilson was born and raised in Campbell, CA, home of the famous Campbell Water Tower.

In January of 2010 he packed his car with everything he owned and 28 hours later arrived in Austin, TX.

Now, in 2018, Bill has a successful real estate business in Austin and is very active in local philanthropic endeavors. His personal slogan—"committed to community"—keeps him highly involved with local non-profits. Along with serving on the 2018 Fete Committee for Ballet Austin and volunteering his photographic work for the Center for Child Protection, Bill has taken photos of shelter dogs at *Austin Pets Alive!* for the past 4+ years, helping hundreds of rescue dogs get adopted. You may have

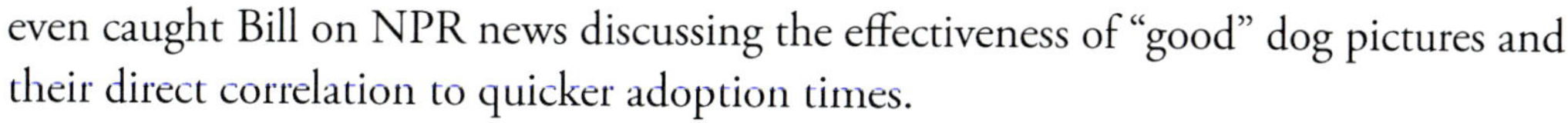

even caught Bill on NPR news discussing the effectiveness of "good" dog pictures and their direct correlation to quicker adoption times.

Bill is a graduate of California State University, Long Beach, with a B.A. in Interpersonal Communication.

He resides in south central Austin with his wife, their daughter, and his two pups, Roxy and Chili, who are *Austin Pets Alive!* alumni!

ACKNOWLEDGMENTS

Thank you first and foremost to Cynthia J. Stone, my literary paladin. From Day 1, your enthusiasm and support provided the medium by which this dream could become a reality.

Gertie June, my loving teammate and wife, thanks for always having my back as we continue this wild journey together.

Dad and Mom, thank you for your endless love. I know I can always count on you. To my brother Jack, thank you for being just a phone call away. I don't know how many times you came out to fix my old pick-up when I'd get stuck somewhere.

John and David, enough can't be said. Thank you for your mentorship, for seeing potential in me and investing the time. Thank you for fueling my passion for photography. It is the camera you gave me that has helped all these wonderful pups find homes.

Thank you to Cherylyn, Tommy, Ginger, Kip, Mattie, Gage, Blain, and Kim. I am beyond blessed that I get to call you my family.

Finally, my appreciation and gratitude goes out to all the hard-working folks at *Austin Pets Alive!* A special thanks to Jess for meeting me countless times in the blistering heat, pouring rain, mud, and even snow to make sure the dogs were ready to have their picture taken.

Made in the USA
Middletown, DE
15 January 2019